Mother of Mercy and of Love

Therese Marie Green

Therese Marie Green

WinePress Publishing
MUKILTEO, WA 98275

Mother of Mercy and of Love
Copyright © 1998 by Therese Green

Published by:
WinePress Publishing
PO Box 1406
Mukilteo, WA 98275

Grateful acknowledgment is made to the Confraternity of Christian Doctrine, Inc., for permission to use scripture texts from the *New American Bible,* copyright 1971, by the Confraternity of Christian Doctrine, Inc., Washington, D.C. 20017-1194. Used by permission of the copyright owner. All rights reserved.

Grateful acknowledgment is made to the Paulist Press for permission to quote from the Dove pamphlet #105 "Healing Relationships with the Miscarried, Aborted and Stillborn Babies" containing material excerpted from *Healing The Greatest Hurt*, by Dennis and Matthew Linn, S.J. and Sheila Fabricant, Paulist Press, © 1985 by the Wisconsin Province of the Society of Jesus and Sheila Fabricant.

Printed in the United States of America.

Library of Congress Catalog Card Number: 97-61752
ISBN 1-57921-058-9

Mother of Mercy and of Love, O Maria

Model of Hope and Encouragement

To Our Lady and
Saints Joachim and Ann
her parents

This statue of St. Joachim with his daughter Mary as a young child, looking to her father, is located in a niche in the arch over the passageway between Our Lady's Chapel and the west transept in the Cathedral of St. Matthew the Apostle in Washington, DC, U.S.A.

Photograph by Carmen C. Figueroa. Used with permission.

This statue of St. Ann with her daughter Mary is located outside the side entrance to St. Ann's Church at Tenley Circle in Washington, DC, U.S.A.

Photograph by Carmen C. Figueroa. Used with permission.

ACKNOWLEDGEMENTS

The author wishes to express her thanks and appreciation to:

- Those who have asked her to pray with them,

- Those who have given financial assistance, especially Peter and Cathy Winter of Bethesda, Md., which made it possible for her to devote so much time to the ministry of intercessory prayer,

- Monina Malixi and Michael Taylor for editorial suggestions,

- Monica Hebert for multiple typing,

- The Rector of St. Matthew's Cathedral, the Pastors of St. Stephen the Martyr and St. Ann parishes, and the Director of St. Ann's Infant and Maternity Home for permission to use photographs of their art works,

- Carmen C. Figueroa and Michael Taylor for photography,

- Patricia Hagy and Mary Ann Hoffman for proofreading, and

- Carolyn Barnes and the students of her 1994 Fourth Grade class at St. John Baptist de la Salle Elementary School in Chillum, Maryland, for their prayers.

May God bless them abundantly.

Contents

FOREWORD

⁓

The full title for this book, *Mother of Mercy and of Love, O Maria Model of Hope and Encouragement,* came to me in 1992 while I was on my way to attend the Mass and prayer vigil held at the Basilica of the National Shrine of the Immaculate Conception, located in Washington, DC, the capital city of the United States of America, on the eve of the Annual Interdenominational March for Life.

The Annual Interdenominational March for Life was begun in 1974, the year after the United States Supreme Court decided *Roe v. Wade.* This decision legalized abortion in the United States. The purpose of this March, according to Nellie Gray, its Founder, is "to educate Americans about the humanity of unborn children." Unless the anniversary of *Roe v. Wade* falls on a Saturday or Sunday, the March is held on January 22nd, the date of this decision. The Vigil Mass, followed by an evening of prayer at the Basilica and a closing Mass at the conclusion of the March the next day, was begun in 1979.

The March officially begins with participants gathering behind the White House, the President's home, to offer and listen to words of counsel regarding the right to life. The March proceeds from the gathering place along Constitution Avenue, named for the document containing the Bill of Rights including the right to life, to the Supreme Court. As they walk, participants offer prayers for a change in the minds and hearts of those who yet believe in the right to choose an abortion, a change similar to that which took place in the minds and hearts of the people who have shared their stories here. Participants then disperse to visit the offices of their elected officials in Congress to ask them to support legislation protecting all human life from the moment of conception to natural death.

The March is led by representatives of several religious denominations and organizations. Participants include a broad cross-section of people. Observers, as well as some protesters, gather outside office buildings along the route.

Prayer services and Eucharists for lost and missing children and their survivors are routinely celebrated publicly and privately in various locations and churches throughout the year. Prayers of reconciliation and healing might also be said. The prayers contained herein are similar to those said at such services.

This photograph is of a stained glass window in the chapel of St. Ann's Infant and Maternity Home, Hyattsville, Maryland, U.S.A. In 1860, the Daughters of Charity opened St. Ann's to care for foundlings and infant orphans and to provide for unprotected females during their confinement in childbirth. St. Ann's continues in this service to this day. The Home also has prenatal residential care programs and a Mother-Baby program in which young mothers stay in residence to learn parenting skills while they continue their education.

Photograph by Carmen C. Figueroa. Used with permission.

INTRODUCTION

Revelations 12:11 states: "They defeated him [the accuser, Satan] by the blood of the Lamb and the word of their testimony." This book contains personal testimonies prepared by people who have experienced God's healing through prayer. These people offered to share the miracle of re-creation in Christ to which their lives give witness to encourage others to accept God's invitation to restoration in the person of His Son Jesus which He extends to all.

Prayers are offered only as suggestions of how a person might open his or her woundedness to Christ and bring the deep hurt of personal loss, whatever its root, to His compassion. Experiencing Christ's acceptance and comfort they might be able to let themselves be healed and in the process become healing love for others.

Although learning may occur, this book is not meant to be one of teaching. It is primarily one of witness and prayer. The book is offered to reassure those who have been affected by deep loss, especially that caused by abortion, that solace, reconciliation and healing are available to all in the Body of Christ.

These stories remind the reader that God's accepting love entices all His children into the fullness of life possible through the power of the cross of Jesus Christ. Christ meets each where that one is and invites the person to enter into and abide in the safety of His Sacred Heart. He gives the gift of His Spirit to draw each one gently and continuously into the Father's heart of love.

The testimonies contained herein are from people I know. They have been blessings in my life. I attest to the accuracy of their witness and the long-standing good fruit their lives currently bear.

It is an unfortunate circumstance that the Body of Christ is broken. Doctrinal and preferential differences abound. All the prayers and suggestions contained herein are Scripture-based and offered in the name of Jesus

Christ. I am a Roman Catholic and my prayer is rooted in the discipline of the Catholic Church. Project Rachel is a ministry within the Catholic Church devoted to helping persons of any faith who are hurting after having been touched by an abortion. My hope is that God will lead people of many faiths to read this book and will bless them through it.

God promises each of us: "See, I make all things new!" (Revelation 21:5) Because of this promise and the truth that God is faithful to His promises, we know that those things which we are willing to surrender to God, will, in His time, be renewed.

Hebrews 4:12 tells us the Word of God is living and effective and has the power to bring about what it says. When we receive God's Word - in the person of Christ, in Scriptures, in Eucharist - into our hearts, we become vulnerable to its power. I pray that we might all read with the anointing and guidance of the Holy Spirit and personally experience God's comfort, love, healing, and blessing in these pages.

I caution you. Although healing, this book can be painful to read. I suggest you begin by reflecting on the fact that we are supported by God's love, that we are precious to Him, and that, no matter what, He loves us. This fact is repeated over and over throughout the book so that, regardless of where the reader begins, God's love will be the focal point for reflection.

For those who will be reading this book alone, it is important to do the things that will help you remember that God is with you and asks you to receive His comfort and peace. For some, this might mean reading in a Church; for others, it might include playing soft, soothing music in the background. Some may benefit from voicing or writing their own prayers. The important thing is to begin exactly where you are and to do whatever you need to do to be and feel safe.

Photographs of statues of Our Lady as a child with her father St. Joachim, her mother St. Ann, the betrothal of Our Lady and St. Joseph, the Holy Family, Jesus with His foster father St. Joseph, and Our Lady as a mature woman are placed throughout the book. These photographs depict the life process: receiving love, nurture, guidance; listening, learning, growing in age, wisdom, and grace.

Mary received such care throughout her life as she matured into the strong woman of

God she became. We can pray that God will place the structure of good parenting within us so we will each, like Mary, come into the fullness of the person God created us to be.

Many books are in print regarding various ways to open oneself to God's healing through prayer. I am happy about this because it helps to guard against creating the impression that a specific method must be used. This is not true. Grace and the Spirit are God's gifts.

Prayers are offered as examples, an outline of sorts, to be used as an aid by someone trying to fashion private prayers. If something in the wording of the prayers does not rest well with you, my suggestion is to skip it and continue. Perhaps this part is not meant for you or the timing is not right. We can trust God to care for each of us without any one of us becoming hurt in the process. The placement of the stories is random. It is not intended to suggest a connection with the specific type of prayer preceding or following. The book can be read in any order. Some might want to read all the stories first and then the prayers. Another might draw strength to read the text and say the prayers by beginning with the section on "Healing the Self Image."

The text begins with three brief diary entries by a pregnant adolescent pressured into having an illegal abortion. Three other testimonies of abortion, woundedness that those involved attribute in large part to the abortions, and healing in and through the Person and cross of Jesus Christ are included. The second story is authored by a woman who had an abortion while in her twenties and subsequently married the father of the aborted child. The third is by a woman who was involved with a married man when she was in her 30's and routinely aborted their children. The fourth is by a man who fathered a child and financed the baby's abortion. The witness of their lives gives honor to God for what He has done and demonstrates the power of prayer to effectuate reconciliation, healing, renewed hope, and a sense of purpose and joy in life.

Beginning Prayer

Let's begin in the name of the Father, and of the Son, and of the Holy Spirit.

My prayer is that all who read this book will place themselves under the protection of the shed blood of Christ and in His Divine Mercy.

May we all know at the deepest level of our beings that we were created out of God's goodness in His image and likeness and we are good. We have always been loved and cherished by our Heavenly Father.

This Father welcomes, accepts, forgives, restores, and blesses us through the merits of His Son, our Brother Jesus.

Nothing we can do changes that.

May we receive Christ's healing and answer His invitation to live safely in His Sacred Heart.

This statue of Our Lady as a young adolescent listening to and learning from her mother St. Ann is located in an outside courtyard at St. Ann's Church, in Washington, DC, U.S.A.

Photograph by Carmen C. Figueroa. Used with permission.

FIRST STORY

❧

February 2, 1975—I feel the "living one" inside me . . . "my Little one" as I call it and I talk to it once I have the time to . . . "Little one, I know you're inside me. I feel your little heart beating . . . beating with love because you are made out of love. Soon you will grow and you will be up and about in this world where I live. I will raise you in selfless love, discipline, understanding and care. You will be intelligent for I will teach you a lot of the world and humanity . . . I will share with you my experiences few though they may be. You will grow to be like me and like him. Perhaps you will get his big brawny muscles, his nice clean smile, his patience and deter-

27

mination, his tact in business if you'll be a he, or my lashes, my red beautiful toes, my straight legs, my tact and creativity ... I'm sure you'll talk a lot too and you'll want to have your way although you'll be less stubborn if you'll be a she. You know something, Little one? I'd love to have you and I want you with me. Someday I'm sure I'll be proud of you and of myself because I know I came to the right decision and that is to keep you. I will never deprive you of your right to live and be part of this world. I love you Little one ... go on living inside me. And when you're all ready to be part of this world, I'll be around to assure you . . . , to say we can make it together . . . you and I.

March 8, 1975—I've had my share of the ups of life . . . such beautiful and happy memories that I shall always treasure in my heart. It is but fair that I get my share of downs now. How I shall face it will determine whether I will be a failure in life or not. The hardest thing in life is not so much the acceptance of the inevitable but having to make a decision. Now I know how it feels to be crushed between two stones, to be pulled by two forces—my family and my baby—which one should I choose? Everything seems to be against my Little one. There seems to be countless disadvantages to having my Little one and yet deep down inside me I know it has the right . . . every right to live.

March 11, 1975—My Little one is gone.

This woman received the Sacrament of Reconciliation and healing prayers in 1986. She is still personally unable to write her story but was willing to share the entries she had made in her diary at the time.

OPENING PRAYER

To receive God's grace, we need to let God know we will open ourselves to receive it. We do this by telling God we are willing to be blessed.

To begin the process of opening to God's grace, it is useful to remember the Divine Exchange that took place in the Garden of Gethsemane and on the cross. We could envision ourselves in the Garden while this is happening. We thereby acknowledge what Scripture tells us—that we are all equal before God (Galatians 2:6). Each of us is someone for whom Christ chose to align His will with that of God the Father and submit to the cross. Thus we all have the same right to claim the full victory gained on that cross for our lives. We can live in that victory by repenting of, confessing, and receiving forgiveness for our sins. Recognizing that Christ died for each of us helps us to believe that He will, indeed, turn our sadness into joy for us (Psalm 126) if we let Him.

We know that God inhabits the praises of His people. Many people recommend praising God as a good way to begin to pray. This can seem awkward to someone unaccustomed to formulating personal prayers. The best thing to do in this case is to keep the words simple and talk directly to God. Some examples are:

I praise You, God. I worship You, God. Be exalted, God. You are my All. Thank you God.

Or, if these are too difficult, examples of others that might feel more honest are:

God, be with me. Help me to want to know You as You truly are. God, help me to want to praise You. Help me to want to love You. Help my soul to long for You. Help me to want to thank You and not blame You.

Then, *"You are my Lord," "I praise You," "Lord, I worship You," "I thank You,"* become easier to say.

Praising God helps us to lift our minds and hearts to God; to focus on Him and His love, rather than on ourselves or our situations. Prayers of praise also help us to develop and maintain a disposition of worship and gratitude. Once the mind and heart begin to turn toward God, the person can move into prayers of thanksgiving. In this, we follow God's own advice contained in 1 Thessalonians 5:16–18: "Rejoice always, never cease praying, render constant thanks; such is God's will for [us] in Christ Jesus."

Prayers of gratitude might go something like this:

Thank you, God the Father,
for the gift of life
this very moment
this day
those I know
and for the healing You offer me in Your
Son Jesus.
I come to You in His name, Lord,
to give You honor and glory.

I thank You, Lord, for telling me
that You have loved me from all eternity
that You have created me lovable

33

*that You always love me
with an everlasting love
regardless of my thoughts and actions.*

*Thank you, God,
for sending Your Son Jesus
to be with us on earth,
to reconcile us to You
and Your perfect love, and
to teach us how to live.*

*I know that You invite me
to be reconciled to Yourself
by my admitting that I am a sinner.
You ask me to accept Jesus
and the healing power of His love,
His forgiveness and the reconciliation
purchased by His shed blood.*

*Thank you, Lord, for telling me
that by Christ's wounds,
I am indeed healed.*

*I come with faith and confidence
to place my own woundedness
into His woundedness
and receive the healing
that He purchased for me on the cross.*

Jesus said to his disciples:

"Go into the whole world
and proclaim the gospel to every creature.
Whoever believes and is baptized will be saved;
whoever does not believe will be condemned.
These signs will accompany those who believe:
    in my name they will drive out demons,
    they will speak new languages.
    They will pick up serpents with their hands,
    and if they drink any deadly thing, it will not harm them.
    They will lay hands on the sick, and they will recover."

So then the Lord Jesus, after he spoke to them, was taken up into heaven
and took his seat at the right hand of God.
But they went forth and preached everywhere,
while the Lord worked with them and confirmed the word through accompanying signs.

James Kotras • kotrasj@stmaryhc.org
Maintenance Supervisor (ext. 153)

Lisa Fox • foxl@stmaryhc.org
Parish Administrative Assistant (ext. 220)

Anne Wycklendt • wycklendta@stmaryhc.org
Parish Administrative Secretary and Bulletin Editor (ext. 250)

Vivian Roe • roev@stmaryhc.org
Parish Accountant (ext. 221)

Nancy Schwemmer • schwemmern@stmaryhc.org
Financial Administrative Assistant (ext. 223)

Jacque Kelnhofer • kelnhoferj@stmaryhc.org
Safe Environment Coordinator (ext. 246)
Administrative Assistant to Liturgy (ext. 246)

Michelle Mroczenski • mroczenskim@stmaryhc.org
Parish School Administrative Assistant (ext. 228)

Kim Jones • jonesk@stmaryhc.org
Parish School Administrative Secretary (ext. 225

registration is required
, First Eucharist Preparation,
enrollment in Catholic Formation
grams.

Infant Baptism

elebrated generally on the second and fourth
e month at 1:00 and 2:00 pm (two families per
lease contact the Parish Office during the first
aptism preparation work is required for parents.

The Sacrament of Matrimony

ent of Matrimony may be celebrated most Fridays
ys of the year, with the exception of the Seasons
d Lent. The bride or the groom or both must be
s members of the parish and are expected to be
ass regularly. Weddings must be scheduled at
onths before the actual wedding date. For more
schedule a wedding, please contact the pastor.

Pastoral Care Ministry

ng to have surgery or if you suddenly take ill and

Help me to welcome this time
of reconciliation and healing.
Thank you.

Please strengthen my belief
in God the Father, my Creator,
in the power of God the Son,
my Redeemer's cross
and resurrection,
and in the anointing of the Holy Spirit,
my Sanctifier.

Thank you, Father,
for making it possible for me to walk
hand in hand
with my brother Jesus
living daily His resurrected glory
His redeemed humanity.

In Jesus' name
I make an act of will
to open myself to God's grace.

Thank you, God, for caring personally
for me.

I pray that none of my attitudes
will interfere with
what You want to do for me

or how You want to heal me.

I will to trust You
with my doubt,
my disbelief, my wounds.

I repent of my failure
to thank You God for my gifts;
my own failure to cherish,
nurture and appreciate these gifts;
and my failure to use them
in Your service to Your honor and glory.

I ask Jesus Christ to intercede
on my behalf
and for all reading this book
as we pray
to heal the diffuse woundedness caused
by abortion,
to end abortion and all senseless de-
struction of life,
to end child abuse and self abuse,
to end the many ways we denigrate
our own lives and those of others.

I ask to bathe in Christ's love
and to be healing love for others.

SECOND STORY

❧

I lay on my bed looking out the back window of my apartment. I was trying to take in the news that I had just received that I was pregnant by my boyfriend of three years. Before I could take it in, the phone rang. It was my best friend calling. I told her, and her response was, "There is a girl in my office who knows the phone number of a doctor in another state who does abortions. It costs $500, and I'll loan you the money." Although abortions were not then legal in the United States, it was settled. I told my boyfriend nothing.

On the day of the abortion, two of my friends accompanied me, although the doctor would not let them wait in the office. He was drunk and molested me. I objected; he went on with the abortion. He told me the baby was a boy. I was emotionally numb throughout the whole time. That abortion is a major spiritual event is attested to by the fact that my boyfriend, who lived in another city, called me the next day to say he had a feeling that something terrible had happened to me. I had stayed home from work, but told him it was nothing serious. I myself felt nothing. I had grown up in an atmosphere of rage, verbal abuse, strict control, and domination and had long ago lost touch with my true feelings. I learned to stuff them down, endure, and go on. I put the abortion behind me.

In another year I married my boyfriend. It wasn't until three years later, when he was developing a drinking problem, that I told him of the abortion in the hope of getting his attention for our relationship. He received the news with seriousness and cut down on his drinking. He felt I had done the right thing to have an abortion to protect our relationship.

I had fallen away from the Catholic Church, and I believed the church would not forgive the sin of abortion even if I confessed it. After ten years of marriage, God very gently and gradually began to draw me back to

Himself and to give me a desire to return to church. For two years I went to Mass without receiving Eucharist. Finally, I decided I should at least try to go to confession. It was Easter weekend when I got up the courage. I prayed beforehand to God and told Him that I didn't want to just confess this sin casually, that I would like to feel sorrow for it. To my surprise, I was flooded with such intense grief that I could not speak; I had to whisper my confession. My confessor was a visiting priest who also whispered and received me gently and lovingly. I stayed in church awhile afterward and went home to find some noisy friends had dropped by. I was aware I had to leave the special place I was in to respond to them.

From that day, God's life grew in me. Soon I became a member of a prayer group and tried to live each day by centering my life on God. My marriage was good and we had two wonderful children. As time went on, I discovered, with the help of a priest friend, strong barriers to love and freedom in my heart. He introduced me to a woman to whom God had given the gift of healing prayer. The three of us met to pray together. As we began to pray, she asked me how many children I had. I said, "Two." She said, "Only two?" And then I remembered the aborted child, which had been forgotten by me, but revealed to her by the Holy Spirit.

The next time the three of us met for prayer, this woman prayed with me to be reconciled with my unborn child. When she asked what I saw in prayer, the Holy Spirit gave me the image of a young boy with curly blond hair. That concurred with what she saw. She asked me his name. I had not named the child, but somehow I knew his name was John. She confirmed this. I was amazed as I did not usually have images or receive information in prayer.

A flood of grief and loss filled my heart. I wanted to ask the child, "Are you all right?" And to ask his forgiveness, too. We spiritually baptized the baby naming him John. As the three of us continued the prayer, I pictured the child growing up in the company of Jesus and Mary, playing with them, and being loved by them. My priest friend then offered a Mass of healing and reconciliation for us. Afterward I felt as if a weight had been lifted from my spirit. And my son, instead of being "an abortion," became a person to me. I found I would from time to time ask him to join me in prayer for the needs of our family.

Forgiving myself for the abortion was still a process, as was accepting God's forgiveness. Once I was on a retreat conducted by a different woman who had a very close relationship with God. During the healing service, she said, "There's a woman here who has had an abortion and can't believe she is forgiven. God wants her to know she is forgiven." And though there was a large crowd in the room, the woman looked kindly in my eyes as she said that.

I have truly experienced Jesus as the Good Shepherd coming after me, His very lost sheep. I have experienced the power of the blood of His covenant to set me free from darkness and bondage. He had been most merciful to send my friend the priest and the two gifted women into my life to bring me to reconciliation and healing. And in the words of Scripture: "I am sure of this much: That he who has begun the good work in [me] will carry it through to completion, right up to the day of Christ Jesus." (Philippians 1:6)

This statuary is located in The Wedding Chapel in St. Matthew's Cathedral, Washington, DC, U.S.A. It is described there as follows:

"The scene portrayed in the statuary represents the betrothal of Our Lady and St. Joseph.

God the Father is represented above the group. The rays descending from Him signify that the High Priest officiating at the betrothal receives his powers and authority from God.

The bearded, older man at the right is St. Joachim. The young man at the far right is breaking a rod, symbolizing the transition from the Old to the New Testament.

St. Ann, the mother of Mary, is the central figure in the group at the left. She is accompanied by the other wedding guests.

The statuary, which is made of sculptured wood overlaid with gold leaf, was designed by Vicenzo Demetz and sons of Artiseic, Italy. Robert Robbins designed the altar."

Photograph by Carmen C. Figueroa. Quotation and photograph used with permission.

SURRENDERING PRAYER

The initial step toward healing is always our admission of our need for healing. For some, a first step indicating the willingness to change is needed. An act of will opens the door to this healing.

For God to change our sadness into joy for us we need to be willing to acknowledge and surrender this sadness to Him. It is useful to begin with a simple prayer like the following:

> *Lord, I choose to repent of my sins. I likewise choose to forgive those who have sinned against me. In the name of Jesus, I choose to forgive myself for sinning against and rejecting parts of myself.*

...k You, Lord, to heal anyone I have ...nned against, and to heal me of woundedness from my own sins. Please heal the wounds I carry from sins committed against me and the effects of the sins of my ancestors. I forgive my ancestors for these sins and on their behalf, I choose to forgive those who sinned against my ancestors.

Many people who have participated in abortions carry deep, deep wounds of self-hate. These wounds most probably pre-date the abortion. People come to hate themselves by taking on the messages of unacceptability they have received from the world and those around them. Unfortunately, these messages come to shape their self-identity. They lose sight of the fact that their identity as God's creatures in His own image and likeness and His adopted children by baptism remains constant as does His steadfast love and acceptance of each and all.

Many who suffer from the aftermath of abortion believe they have done the worst possible thing they could have done, and have become nothing. Their lives have become worthless. Having taken life, they think they no longer have the right to exist or enjoy life.

Regardless of whether woundedness from an abortion is present, God invites all of us to surrender any ideas such as these to Him, and to let Him begin to lift them from our minds, hearts, and spirits.

God is calling us to let Him change any attitudes we carry that are not in accord with His will, His Word, His call. He asks us to surrender to Christ's cross any beliefs and feelings that stand between us and His love for us. These include all sense of inadequacy, futility, dejection, utter hopelessness and helplessness, as well as ideas that God has abandoned us.

One attitude that particularly inhibits our ability to experience spiritual healing is a belief that God cannot possibly forgive us for what we have done. This attitude makes it impossible for us to receive the forgiveness God offers us or to forgive ourselves.

Beginning with a decision of our wills to permit God to heal us in these areas opens our minds and hearts to re-creation. We might fashion a prayer like this:

In the name of Jesus, I agree to repent of self-hatred.

Lord, I choose to receive Your Word in place of those self-destructive words now written in my own heart.

I choose to believe that You do love me
that You have always loved me
that You created me lovable
that You want me to love myself
and to let others love me.

I choose to believe
that there is nothing I did,
or could ever do,
that would cause You
to stop loving me,
and that You do want to bless me.

After having made an act of will to permit God to heal us, we ask Him to change our hearts—to place His own forgiveness, compassion, and mercy towards us and others within our hearts.

As we continue in an attitude of listening prayer and openness to the Holy Spirit, God will bring areas of our hearts to our awareness and let us choose whether we are ready to surrender them to the redeeming power of Christ's cross. This is God's work; we rest in His love and let Him accomplish

it in us in His time. Our prayer might go
something like this:

*I again give You permission, Lord, to
change my heart regarding myself.*

*I ask You, Lord,
to help me relinquish to You
the ways I chose to shut out
or close down
in response to circumstances in my life.*

*Lord, I surrender the ways
that I have interfered
with Your creation of me and others,
the choices that I have made,
that were outside Your will.
I repent of these sins and
ask Your forgiveness.*

*I ask, Lord,
that You would begin to remove
those structures I have built
within myself
which interfere with
my becoming
that perfect image
God the Father had of me
when He created me.*

*I give You permission
to take me by the hand
and look with me
through those doors
which are now opening
in the safety of Your embrace
the doors in those walls
that I built to protect myself
from further hurt
when I felt
so alone, sad, scared, and vulnerable.*

*I know that gently,
with Your love,
You will coax me back
into the fullness of the life
God the Father
always intended for me.*

*I thank You
that You do welcome me
with loving arms
and take me to God my Father.*

*Jesus, I bring to You
my sense of nothingness—
that internal void.
I ask You to place Your shed blood
at the very point*

of my perceived nothingness.

Please enter into
this point of separation,
this split from my sense of being,
my sense of wholeness,
my sense of integrity.

Lord, I ask
that You would pour
Your redeeming shed blood into
those areas of division and separation,
filling them
and resurrecting them
to a life of Easter promise,
hope and joy.

Lord, I acknowledge
that I have not valued
and cherished my own life
or the lives of those people
whom You have placed in my path,
whom You gave into my charge.

Jesus, I likewise place
these attitudes against myself,
against all Your people, and
against You

into Your wounds,
into Your Divine Mercy,
into Your Sacred Heart,
that they might be transformed
into what You would have them be.

I ask You to change my heart
to give me a heart of flesh,
to re-symbolize love and life for me,
to give me a loving, compassionate and
merciful heart—
to recreate a right spirit in me.

Please align my heart and mind with
Your divine plan.
Thank you.

THIRD STORY

It was a warm evening in June 1988 but I had felt a strange chill in my bones all day and had wrapped myself in a blanket for warmth. I was curled up on the floor of my apartment, dozing off. I had spent the afternoon weeping. Somehow I knew what my problem was. I was suffering the aftermath of multiple abortions. I had my first abortion on November 19, 1977. From then to 1983, I had four more.

In the spring of 1975 I became involved with a married man. We discussed the possibility of having children. Although he assured me that he would stand by me in the unlikely event that I became pregnant, inasmuch as I was taking birth control pills, I knew that—as the other woman—I was on my own. I was also afraid that children would further complicate an already complicated situation and, if that happened, the man would eventually leave me. The thought of losing him was unbearable.

I missed my period in September 1977, and before I even went to see a doctor, I knew that I was pregnant. I could sense a change in my body. I was terrified and immediately entertained thoughts of abortion. I needed so much to talk to someone; but, at the same time, I was afraid to confide in anyone. The fear of condemnation and rejection, especially by my family, was so strong. How would I survive? What if I lost my job? How would I support the baby?

I finally mustered enough courage to confide in a girlfriend who I heard had had an abortion. She gave me an address and also agreed to accompany me the next day.

My friend and I reached the lady's house by mid-morning. The woman immediately gave me a tranquilizer. Then she prepped me for a D&C. I was covered with sweat and screaming from the pain. As she scraped off the last of my baby's body into a basin, I remember thinking over and over, "Forgive me." When she finished, she came around the side of the bed to show me what was in the basin as proof, she said that she "had taken everything out." I turned my face away, sobbing all the while, praying for my poor baby. I watched her walk away with the basin, and, in my mind, I said a last prayer and baptized my dead child.

I knew I had sinned against God and through the pain in my body and spirit, I screamed out for forgiveness. In my selfishness and ignorance, I also expected relief afterwards. As an unmarried woman, I had considered my pregnancy a problem and the solution I sought was abortion. Sure, I felt relief afterwards, relief from the sleepless nights of worry about the consequences of having a child out of wedlock; relief that now, after the abortion, I could go on with my life as if nothing had happened.

But something else came along with that relief, something strange and heretofore unknown to my spirit. Something insidious and alien which finally planted itself firmly into my whole being, like a conquering enemy. I had no name for it at the time, except Depression. There was a numbness, a deadness in my spirit that robbed me of the ability to enjoy life from that point on. In murdering my unborn child, I had killed my own spirit.

I went through a personality change shortly after that first abortion. Initially, the change became apparent at home. I became hypersensitive and melancholy; alternatively abusive and withdrawn. In the workplace, the situation was the same. I was hurting so much inside that I kept everyone at bay by becoming increasingly obnoxious and abrasive.

Two years later, my boyfriend voiced his concern about my prolonged use of the Pill. I had developed cysts in my breasts and, although they were diagnosed as benign, my doctor advised me to have them surgically removed. He also intimated that one probable cause was the Pill. I decided to take his advice and shortly afterwards I became pregnant with my second child. This time I told my boyfriend about the pregnancy and he found a lady physician who agreed to perform the abortion. We went to see her at her clinic. After taking our money, she took me into a private room for the procedure. My boyfriend waited outside. The doctor told me that she would use a suction to extract the fetus and that it would be virtually painless. However, during the procedure, the instrument malfunctioned and she said she had to perform a D&C instead. I was into labor by then and, when I saw her falter with the instrument, I began to panic. There was no time to wait for the anesthesia to take effect and I screamed in agony as waves of pain engulfed my body. I must have passed out because when I came to consciousness, my boyfriend was in the room with me.

My relationship with my boyfriend began to change in little, subtle ways as we both underwent changes in our personalities. He became withdrawn and morose. Although I was never the target of his anger, he became more and more abrasive and antagonized even his closest friends.

The last three abortions I had were done with saline solution injections. They were relatively painless. I was keenly aware of what was taking place in my body, in my womb. I "felt" my babies die. One I remember profoundly. I "felt" when my child's heartbeat actually stopped. And it stopped with a wrenching contraction of my own heart. At first I thought I was having a heart attack because I felt a strange irregular heartbeat, and an eerie sense of two hearts beating. One was my own, which was beating quite normally, and then there was another one, beating at a rising staccato as if in a panic. Then, I felt the heart go into slow wrenching spasms, like when someone is gasping for air. Then, it began to slow down. Then, stop.

Two years after my last abortion, I ended the relationship. I found absolutely no meaning in life and several times contemplated suicide. I socialized less and less because I no longer enjoyed other people's company. I felt loneliest when I was in a crowd and had difficulty interacting with people. If people talked about children, I would start to feel uncomfortable and quietly withdraw into myself or simply leave. If I managed to join in the conversation, my responses sounded hollow and phony to my ears. I averted my eyes when children came into view. I lived alone, my day consisting of early morning Mass and work. My weekends were spent taking long walks until I got so tired I would drop, but I suffered from chronic insomnia and got no rest at night.

Eleven years after my first abortion, thoughts of ending my life became a constant companion. I contemplated buying a gun for protection. The city was not a safe place to live in, I rationalized, and I lived alone. But some inner voice warned me against buying the gun. Somehow, I had a vague sense that if I had a gun in the house, ultimately I would put it to my head.

I knew that only God could give me the peace I yearned for. Although I had asked

God's forgiveness in prayer for my sins, I had not been to the Sacrament of Reconciliation for almost 20 years. I asked a girlfriend to help me find a priest. She referred me to her father confessor and also suggested that I speak with a woman who was well known in the healing prayer ministry. I went to see this wonderful priest who walked me through reconciliation with God with utmost compassion and kindness. He also suggested that I see the same woman for healing prayers.

At the first prayer session I had with this woman, when she laid hands on me and prayed, I sensed a strong and immediate change in my spirit. It was my first experience of healing prayer. I felt strengthened in my inner core and immediately experienced a deeper need to pray. I knew God was showing me then that prayer was His way of healing me. Shortly thereafter, I went to a *Life in the Spirit* seminar and was baptized in the Spirit. Through subsequent prayer sessions with this woman, I slowly but surely began to grow in the Spirit. More importantly, the powerful witness of her own prayer life and spiritual journey has enriched my own walk with Christ.

I had a Mass of Reconciliation said for my children, during which I baptized and named them and committed them to the Lord. In this prayer of surrender, I also committed to the Lord my love for my children. Each day I pray that He continues to bless, purify and transform that love into His own and that we may continue to love one another through Him.

At the suggestion of this woman, I went to the Sacrament of Reconciliation regularly to the same priest who had ministered to me the first time. This was not because I needed to confess the abortions more than once, but to avail myself of the healing power of the Sacrament of Reconciliation. This spiritual regimen helped me a great deal in processing my personal guilt for the abortions and helped me to forgive myself and to receive the Lord's forgiveness and love.

I try to go to daily Mass and Communion as part of my own spiritual regimen. The Holy Sacrifice of the Mass is the most powerful source of God's healing for me.

My children are dead, but I know they are in heaven with God. That is the only place I want to be when I die—with God, with them. Everyday I try to live my life with that goal in mind. I know with God's grace, I can do it.

RECEIVING PRAYER

God invites us to listen with our hearts to words such as these:

Give Me your wounds,
You do not know how to let them be re-
deemed,
how to let them be used in My service,
as an instrument of My healing love.
I do.

But I will not disturb them without your
consent.

I know that
you have protected them
for a long time,
that you have tried

to ignore their existence,
and some have even tried to make virtues of them.

I ask you
to bring them to Me now
that I might redeem and restore,
that you might become
what My and Your Father
intended for you to be
from the beginning of all time.

I call you forth
and ask you to step out of
your despair and desolation.

I ask you to step out of
your sense of defilement and shame.
I ask you to step out of
your self-contempt, scorn,
and hatred for all humanity,
and step into My heart
of love and hope for you.

God Our Father created
humanity beautiful
and He declared it very good.

*You are good by the very fact of having
been created (Genesis 1:31).*

*I offer you
the opportunity to see yourself as whole
the way Our Heavenly Father sees you.
I receive you into My wounds
that you might be healed (1 Peter 2:24).*

*I ask you
to let go of your own contempt
and hard-heartedness
toward yourself and others
and to receive My love for you.
I invite you to live
in My own compassionate heart.*

*When God created originally,
He called things into existence
out of the void,
and I am calling the void,
the emptiness,
the woundedness
you now feel
to My own wounds
to be cleansed and purified,
that you might be a sturdier vessel in
My kingdom.*

I need you to let Me heal you
at this depth of your being
because, along with You,
the world is in deep need
of this kind of healing.

You understand this depth of pain,
this depth of wretchedness,
this depth of disconnectedness,
this complete and total
feeling of nothingness.

I need you to serve Me.
I need you to serve Me at these depths.
You can become My healing love
in the world at this time.
I need you now.

Please do not deny my requests.

I know there is great pain
in your wounds,
I will hold you
while you experience the pain,
and I will unite it with My own pain,
and it too will become redemptive.

Can you not imagine
that I know the pain

of rejection and abandonment?
Most of My friends left Me on the cross.

This photograph of the Holy Family is of a ceramic in a private collection.

Photograph by Carmen C. Figueroa. Used with permission.

When I saw them again,
I said, "My peace be with you."
This is what I say to you now.

To those areas
that you have kept from Me
that you are afraid to bring to Me,
I say: Come Back.
Welcome Home.

I am seeking you,
I am calling you.
I am bringing you back to Me.
I want to re-form you, to re-shape you,
not to chastise you.

I want to guide you, but, first of all,
I want to comfort you,
I want to enter into your wound
and set things right.
I want to nurse you back to wholeness.

Many of you are suffering
many kinds of difficulties
which you have never traced
to the loss of a child.

I want to enter into those
and heal them now.

Just be still
and know that I am God.
Know that I
can put everything right.

Some of you believe
that you were so ignorant.
Know that I am with you
even in your lack of knowledge.
Again I ask you to surrender
that attitude against yourself
to Me.

Some of you have attempted
to re-connect to life
in all sorts of inappropriate ways.
I understand that.
But,
I ask you
to stop searching everywhere
and just come to Me.

Let Me take you to Our Father
that you might rest
in the security of His love,
that your restlessness would cease,
that you might live in peace.

I am prepared to remove
any fear of pregnancy,
of others,
of relationships,
of sexuality itself
that you might carry.
Just release these fears to Me.

I trust you with life.

This statue of St. Joseph teaching his foster son Jesus to become a carpenter is located in St. Stephen the Martyr Church in Washington, DC, U.S.A.

Photograph by Michael Taylor. Used with permission.

FOURTH STORY

During a period of over twenty years of living in the Hell of alcoholism, I caused a pregnancy in a young woman who lived in another town. I had known her for many years and she was a good friend of my family as I was of hers. When she contacted me, I took a neutral stand toward abortion, and she terminated the pregnancy. We did not communicate again for years. During my later recovery from alcoholism the stark reality of this tragedy really struck home; but I initially wrote it off as "one of those things that happens to alcoholics." I did not consciously think about the abortion and did nothing to reconcile myself to my unborn child nor to its mother, who later married and had a stillborn infant as her first child.

About fifteen years after the abortion, I was weighed down with an unusual amount of guilt. I had even resorted to several different kinds of treatments to find relief from this sense of sin and unworthiness. During all this time I was receiving the Sacraments of the Catholic Church regularly. I had never married and my relationships with women were in general unsatisfactory, never lasting more than several months before I would abruptly terminate them. With the advent of sobriety from alcohol, these relationships became mostly non-intimate, but still very empty and non-spiritual.

At this point God providentially put into my life two laypeople who had a ministry of healing prayer. They helped me deal with a mountain of spiritual ills, which I had never been able to resolve. Among these were hatred and bitter judgments against my parents; rejection of discipline; deceit in the form of exaggeration and lying; gross sensuality, extending to personal sex and excessive eating and drinking. I had also learned that my mother had tried to abort me; she was pregnant out of wedlock.

The healing prayer proceeded over several months and included seeking healing for the abortion, to which I had tacitly consented, and reconciliation with my baby. I realized I had never formally confessed this sin. In the course of the healing prayers, I also came to realize that periodic nightmares I had over the years that featured a shriveled child locked inside a furnace had nothing to do with my own sad childhood but rather with my unreconciled baby.

Following the procedures recommended by the Linn brothers in their Paulist Press pamphlet, *Healing Relationships With Aborted Babies,* after Confession, I attended Eucharist and joined Jesus in praying that my child and I might be drawn closer to Him forever. In this Eucharist of Reconciliation, I also asked Jesus to extend His love to other aborted children who may have been forgotten, including the 4,000 aborted daily in this country. At the conclusion of this Eucharist, I experienced the sentiments of a woman named Elizabeth (cited in the Linn brothers' pamphlet) who had had an abortion and expressed her feelings thus after being reconciled with her child and with God the Father: "My biggest release came in my love for the Father. The loosening of anger from my heart, mind and spirit freed me to receive more of His love. That love flooded me with a depth of joy I had never experienced before."

I chose the name Matthew for my child and spiritually baptized him to let Jesus wash away all the hurt that had been done to my child by me, the child's mother, the abortionist, and all who had contributed to his death. Again following the Linn brothers' recommendation, I then spiritually placed the newly baptized Matthew into the arms of Jesus and Mary. Matthew, after being warmly received by them, was placed into my arms by a smiling Mary and my child smiled and cooed in a way that brought great tears to my eyes. The withered child of my nightmares was no more.

The next day in my office complex I heard someone inside one of the cubicles say as I walked past: "The child's name should be Matthew." I had no idea who the person was who said this, or what the context of their conversation was. Two days after Matthew's baptism I was sitting in an Alcoholics Anonymous meeting in a church basement. I didn't have my glasses on so I couldn't make out the titles of the books on a distant shelf. Only one was visible, a book with the title *Matthew* in large letters.

When the author of this book approached me with the idea of my contributing, I realized that I have a real spiritual bond with my child who has already preceded me to heaven. The breach brought about by the abortion has been healed, and I pray that my dear son Matthew will intercede for spiritual help and guidance for me on my earthly pilgrimage that I may continue to give to others the love which I failed to show to him at the beginning of his life.

A Special Word for Those Who Have Suffered Miscarriages

God invites us to listen with our hearts to words such as these:

From those who are suffering the loss of little ones through miscarriage, I want to remove the idea that you went through everything you could—but that it was for nothing. That is not true.

I forgive you for your anger toward me.

I ask you to release to Me any attitude that you have that you are not the proper home to nurture new life.

Release to me any sense that you might carry that as a parent you did not welcome the life that I entrusted to your care.

You need not feel any sense of guilt or terrible stigma because of the circumstances of your children's births, because you did not carry them to term.

These babies are with Me. They mature and grow in spirit with Me. These children mature under the blessing and protection of My and Your Heavenly Father.

I have communicated your sorrow to your children. I assure you that they have learned how to forgive from Me.

They have only compassion and love for you in their hearts. I share this with you now.

They are trophies in My kingdom where they pray for you. I honor them as I honor you.

Healing the Self Image

⟋∾⟍

Our God is a God of great compassion and love. He created us out of His goodness and we are good. Regardless of what has happened to us or what we have done, we are created in the image and likeness of God. Nothing can change that.

God is a God of order and harmony. God wants to bring all who are willing to let Him into accord with this order and harmony. One way to pray for this is to place a hand on the upper chest and ask Jesus to come and place order, harmony, integrity, and wholeness into our beings.

We can pray, "*Holy Spirit, let the order of the Lord come in*," and wait for the prayer to settle and take effect. Depending on our response, we can continue by substituting other qualities as the Spirit leads. For instance, we might ask for prudence, justice, solace, patience, comfort, strength, courage, or other virtues to meet whatever needs we are experiencing. Then we can ask God to let these qualities flow in and through us.

Whenever the Holy Spirit enlightens us regarding areas of our hearts that need changing, especially in ways we do not love ourselves appropriately, we can surrender those to be healed and pray for corresponding virtues to replace them. Once again, articulating a conscious choice to permit God to enter these areas as they come to our awareness helps in the surrendering and receiving process.

A simple prayer like the following is all that is needed.

In the name of Jesus,
I choose to forgive myself
for hating myself
and I give You permission, Lord,
to change my heart toward myself.

I ask You, Jesus,
to help me see myself
with Your eyes,
that I might
let You be

what You are
Emmanuel God with me
in the area
of my self-hatred.
Thank you.

Sometimes it is also useful to make an act of will to let God be God His way. God is not going to change. His unchange-ability, especially the unchangeability of His steadfast love for us, makes it possible for us to trust and rest in Him and His authority. It is the stabilizing force upon which we can rely.

Remembering that Jesus is not going to force us to be healed, we can trust the pace of His healing. God does not let anything become known before good can come from it, as long as we cooperate. We can feel safe as we let the Holy Spirit gently move into the areas of our hearts trapped in wrong judgments and attitudes. In situations of deep entrenchment such as self-hatred usually is, it is useful to begin by letting these areas just marinate and thus soften in God's love.

We can ask the Lord to let the Holy Spirit come and rest upon any area of hardness of our hearts towards ourselves, others, the world, and God; especially around any areas of unbelief and mistrust in God's love, care, and providence.

Some people carry within themselves the idea that they can never recover or be healed. God wants to lift that idea and restore their hope.

Others believe that it is all right to ignore things and they will just go away. God is asking us to let Him bring back into our awareness those things which we have chosen to ignore in the past, that He might give us the strength and fortitude to acknowledge them now, surrender them to Him, and let Him make us whole.

Many carry an enormous sense of futility, waste, and loss about their lives. The Lord seeks to fill that depth of despair with His love and reassurance that our lives are in His hands and in His time. He is the God of restoration, hope, and promise of a future.

It is God's truth that sets us free (John 8:32) and heals us. We can begin owning this truth about ourselves by meditating on Scriptures.

CLOSING PRAYER

Let us close this time of prayer and reflection by letting God minister His Word to us as we read through these Scripture passages. Blanks are given to remind us to insert our own names, "I", or "me" and realize that God is speaking to each of us personally. God's Word is alive and active and has the power to effectuate what it says (Hebrews 4:12). Christ is God's Word made flesh. In the person of Christ we are reconciled to the Father. Through the power of the Holy Spirit we are sanctified. By Christ's wounds we are healed (Peter 2:24). By meditating on His Word we are made whole.

"With age-old love I have loved you [   ]; so I have kept My mercy toward you." (Jeremiah 31:3)

"[   ], I, the Lord, am your healer."
(Exodus 15:26)

"Fear not, I am with you [   ]; be not
dismayed; I am your God. I will
strengthen you, and help you, and up-
hold you with My right hand of justice."
(Isaiah 41:10)

"Because you [   ] are precious in My
eyes and glorious, and because I love
you." (Isaiah 43:4)

"I will never forget you [   ]. See, upon
the palms of My hands I have written
your name." (Isaiah 49:15–16)

"By [Christ's] wounds, you [   ] were
healed." (1 Peter 2:24)

"God created man in His image; in the
divine image He created him, male and
female [   ] He created them." (Genesis 1:27)

"God looked at everything He had made
[including   ], and He found it very
good." (Genesis 1:31)

"For I am certain that neither death nor life, neither angels nor principalities, neither the present nor the future, nor powers, neither height nor depth nor any other creature, will be able to separate us [ ] from the love of God that comes to us in Christ Jesus, our Lord." (Romans 8:38–39)

"But now, thus says the Lord, who created you, O Jacob, and formed you, O Israel: Fear not, for I have redeemed you [ ]; I have called you by name: you are Mine." (Isaiah 43:1)

"Fear not, for I am with you [ ]." (Isaiah 43:5)

"I will welcome you [ ] and be a Father to you and you will be My sons and daughters." (2 Corinthians 5:18)

"I have loved you [ ] with an everlasting love; with loving kindness I have drawn you to Me." (Jeremiah 31:3)

"Fear not, for I have redeemed you [ ]; I have called you by name: you are Mine." (Isaiah 43:1–4)

This statue of Our Lady as a mature woman is located in Our Lady's Chapel, St. Matthew's Cathedral, Washington, D.C., U.S.A.

It is described as follows:

"The compassionate figure of the Blessed Virgin serves as the focal point of this Chapel. With her left hand she gestures toward her Son and with her right she welcomes all who would approach her and her Son. The statue is the work of Gordon Kray."

Photograph by Carmen C. Figueroa. Quotation and photograph used with permission.

MAGNIFICAT

∾

Then Mary said:

*"My being proclaims the greatness of
the Lord, my spirit finds joy in God my
Saviour, For He has looked upon His
servant in her lowliness; all ages to
come shall call me blessed. God who is
mighty has done great things for me,
holy is His name; His mercy is from age
to age on those who fear Him."*

(Luke 1:46–50)

AFTERWORD

I have prayed with several others working through the pain of abortion. Many are not ready to share their stories publicly. But all have said that one of the great burdens they carry is the inability to find someone to listen and to hear their stories. It is important that these stories and testimonies to God's love be told to encourage others suffering similar pain and loss to seek and accept the same comfort and healing and restoration in the heart of Jesus.

REVIEWS

✺

"In this book, Ms. Green leads the reader to a refreshing and profound appreciation of the role that prayer serves in healing lives wounded by abortion. Carefully selected stories open a window onto the truth about abortion and how it has impacted particular persons' lives. The reader is gently invited to reflection and prayer. This book is best read slowly and repeatedly. Denial about abortion has become a way of life in our society. Ms. Green's book awakens us from our lethargy and gives us the courage to offer our pain and brokenness to the healing love of a merciful God."

—Michael Taylor, S.T.D., Executive Director; National Committee for a Human Life Amendment

"You did a superb work. I was much honored to have the opportunity to read this material. No doubt the Holy Spirit was with you to inspire the prayers. I can see there is a seed in this book which will pop up and produce great fruits of peace and confidence in the Lord who is always waiting at the door no matter our weakness."

—Philippe Nadeau, M. of Afr.
Brother, Missionaries of Africa

"Amazing grace/How sweet the sound," wrote John Newton after his conversion from plying the slave trade a century ago. This same spectacular, healing love of our God echoes from the stories in this work of Therese Green about the tortured lives of those experiencing, or involved in, abortions. Her own deep spirituality and compassion, emanating from more than fifteen years engaging in a ministry of intercessory prayer, are wonderfully reflected in the long, beautiful prayers throughout this booklet. I have used some of the prayers as part of a daily homily and have had people ask for copies. Might not these powerful cries of the heart be useful to all of us in our brokenness?"

—Rev. Mike Blackwell,
St. Mary's Catholic Church
Landover Hills, MD 20784

"I believe the book Mother of Mercy is a valuable resource for anyone dealing with the spiritual wounds of abortion or for anyone seeking to companion another through this healing. It provides a gentle framework within which to examine the wounds of one's life and bring them before God, the Master Healer."

—Vicki Thorn, Director
National Office of Post-Abortion Reconciliation & Healing, Inc.
1-800-5WE-CARE
Foundress, Project Rachel

ABOUT THE AUTHOR

Therese Green is an attorney. She has clerked at the Eighth Circuit, served as a Bigelow Fellow at the University of Chicago Law School, and engaged in private practice in the international arena. The author worked with the Peace Corps both as an education volunteer in Ethiopia and as a staff member and has served as an international education consultant. She has been active in intercessory prayer ministry for a number of years. She can be contacted at PO Box 596, Mundelein, Illinois 60060.

To order additional copies of

Mother of Mercy and of Love

send $7.99* + $3.95 shipping and handling to:

WinePress Publishing
P.O. Box 1406
Mukilteo, WA
98275

To order by phone, please have your credit
card ready and dial

1-800-917-BOOK

*Quantity discounts available upon request.